A gift for

_____

From

_____

it's a **happy** thing

© 2006 Hallmark Licensing, Inc.

Published by Gift Books from Hallmark,
a division of Hallmark Cards, Inc.,
Kansas City, MO 64141
Visit us on the Web at www.Hallmark.com.

Art Director: Kevin Swanson
Editorial Director: Todd Hafer

Editorial development by Scott Degelman & Associates
Designed by The Pink Pear Design Company, LLC.
Illustrations by Bob Kolar

it's a **happy** thing

A Joyful Collection of
Secrets, Smiles, and Surprises

BOK3078

it's a **happy** thing

What makes you happy?

Watching birds at a feeder or enjoying a rich dessert? The great thing about happiness is that it sprinkles its seeds just about anywhere you look. You can practically go out with a basket and gather joy, like wild blueberries—its delicious juiciness staining your fingers and filling your belly—until you can't possibly take in one more moment of blissful perfection. • The thing is, we all have our own ways of finding happiness. And since happiness makes us feel so good, it's just natural that we want to share it! That's where this book comes in. It's jam-packed with ideas, inspirations, and intriguing thoughts on living a life full of sunshine. So sit back, put on a smile, and enjoy an entire book devoted to the happiest subject on earth.

101

Reasons to Smile

People find happiness in the funniest places, from free refills, to fluffy towels, to high school football games. So what about you? What simple pleasures tickle your toes and delight your days? Here's a list to inspire you...

1 **SUNSETS**

2 High school musicals

3 There's almost always a *Seinfeld* rerun on.

4 Dark chocolate is good for you.

5

free
samples

Johnny Cash

compilations

7 Postage-paid return envelopes

8 Pixar movies
9 Overdraft protection

10 Automated car washes – part labor-saving
convenience, part amusement park ride

11 Even water comes in a variety of flavors now.

12 Somebody has a crush on you,
maybe even a few "somebodies."

13 The memory of your

first kiss

14 There's some loose cash lurking somewhere in your home; you'll find it eventually.

15 # James Taylor

16 Red wine is good for you.

17 Luggage on wheels

18 # Friday
is never that far away.

19 **Bubble gum**

is still fun – and still cheap.

20 They've finally created some energy bars that don't taste like cardboard

21 You can make your hair pretty much any color you want.

22 There's always a chance that boring meeting will get cancelled.

23 High-definition TV

24 Free refills

25 Turns out that eggs aren't really bad for you.

26 **Sunrises**

27 **Bendy straws**

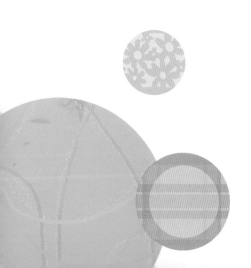

28 Regifting **is still** socially acceptable, if you're discreet.

29 Most elevators don't play elevator music anymore.

Satellite radio

There are seven wonders of the world, not a mere six or five.

32 Computers

keep getting cheaper, lighter, and faster.

33 Our brave women and men in the military

34 Non-greasy lotions

35 John Hughes movies

36 That anti-baldness stuff
is now available over-the-counter.

37 Cameron Crowe movies
(except *Vanilla Sky*, of course)

38 Southwest Airlines staff is a riot.

39 You don't have to pretend to like
foreign films
if you really don't.

40 All of those flavored

coffee
creamers

41 Babies seem to like you.

₄₂ Glasses are in,
and there's a style that will look great on you.

₄₃ Miles Davis

₄₄ Books are still one of the best bargains going.

45 You're still pretty good at

Ping-Pong.

46 Fresh-squeezed

lemonade

47 Green tea,
good and good for you

48 Video-store late fees are becoming extinct.

49 Your signature looks cool;
it would make a great autograph.

50 High school
football games

There will be some great pictures on that old roll of undeveloped film you just found.

52 **garage**

53 **Hello,**
national Do Not Call list;
goodbye, telemarketers.

54 Peanuts comics are timeless,
same with the TV specials.

sales

55 Baby-sitting is still a bargain.

56 You don't live in the pre-dishwasher era.

57 They didn't make a sequel to *Casablanca.*

58 Online bill pay

59 You look a lot better than that celebrity
who just had another plastic surgery.

60 Saltwater taffy is
delicious
(and doesn't actually taste salty).

61 More TV channels
= more choices

62 Caller ID

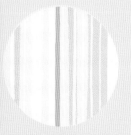

63 Running shoes look cooler than ever.

64 Even McDonald's has some healthful stuff on the menu.

65 There are more coffee flavors than ever— even for people who don't like coffee.

66 The healthful powers of pomegranate juice

67 That pasteurized egg stuff means worry-free cake and cookie batter eating.

68 **Spring** is never that far away.

69 **The Simpsons**

. . . still funny after all these years

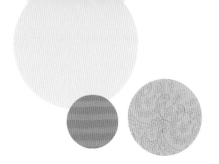

70 Naps are in.
(Call yours a "power nap" if it makes you feel better.)

71 Large-print books

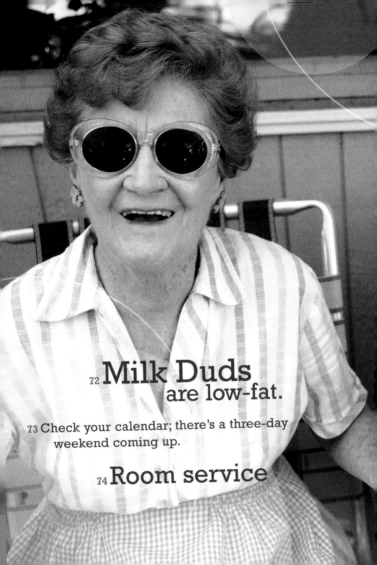

72 **Milk Duds**
are low-fat.

73 Check your calendar; there's a three-day
weekend coming up.

74 **Room service**

75 SportsCenter
is on multiple times every day.

76 It takes 26 muscles to smile;
just think of the workout you'll get
on your "happy days."

77 Bubble wrap
is fun to pop.

78 You can create your own Web site.

79 Black-and-white movies
on late-night TV

80 Your favorite team will have
a better season next year.

81 Your

hair

looks way, way better than Donald Trump's.
(Better than his current wife's, too.)

82 Low-fat ice cream

83 Uncomfortable shoes are out.

84 Self-cleaning ovens

85 Stevie Wonder

86 You can now record favorite TV shows and watch them whenever....

87 That new issue of your **favorite** **magazine** will be in your mailbox soon.

88 Self-stick postage stamps

89 More soda flavors
than ever before

90 Sports
mascots

91 Warm,
fluffy
clothes and towels,
fresh
from the dryer

92Johnny Carson-era
Tonight Show episodes on DVD

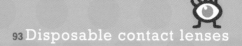

93 Disposable contact lenses

94 Fresh-squeezed
orange juice

95 The kids in your life like Dylan
and Zeppelin as much as you do.

96 iPods,
all kinds of iPods

97 You could be eating hot

popcorn

in about five minutes.

98 **Used-book stores**

99 Someone you know and love
made the Honor Roll.

100 **You still have
some sick days left.**

101 That thing you've been trying to recall? Don't worry; it'll come back to you.

Kids

on Happiness

According to the Discovery Health Web site,
children laugh an average of 300 times a day,
while the average adult laughs only 17 times
daily. What do kids know about happiness that
adults are missing? Read on and find out...

Happiness is...

A choice.
James, age 15

Being me.
Chris, age 13

Having more than enough
and sharing it.
Cassie, age 14

Cool.
Isaiah, age 12

Living joyfully with the people you love—with no one judging anyone else.

JJ, age 14

Available to us all.
Carrie, age 15

Mine!
Donny, age 6

My mom!
Sergio, age 7

Caring about others.
Ashley, age 16

Just being yourself.
Monique, age 12

Money!
Michael, age 8

Focusing on the good stuff.
Brittany, age 15

The people who love me.

Kevin, age 9

My dog!

Whitney, age 5

Giving.

Cyndi, age 10

Happiness
doesn't have anything
to do with money.
It's about bringing
some **joy**
into the world.

Lily, age 9

Being who God made you.
Christian, age 12

Being thankful.
Dominic, age 11

Not stressing out.
Rory, age 13

Right here.
Gabriel, age 14

Knowing God.
Ryan, age 9

My family.
Patricia, age 12

Hearing 'Good job!'

Travis, age 12

Hearing 'I love you.'

Jessica, age 11

Feeling
loved.

Solomon, age 5

Being kind to others.

Charles, age 8

Happiness is what my mom has
when I clean the house for her.

Jennifer, age 14

Liking what
you have.
Martina, age 13

Hugs!

Taylor, age 4

Happiness is...being happy.
Bryce, age 7

Joking and laughing a lot.
Gary, age 10

My toys!
Jay, age 3

Happiness is enjoying yourself,
thinking about **happy times**
instead of bad times;
thinking about
the interesting things
you like to do.

AJ, age 13

Happiness is giving.
Brennan, age 8

Trusting God.
Marissa, age 12

Happiness is
boats &
choo-choos.

Silas, age 3

Having what you need.
Martin, age 10

Cherishing good memories.
Brandon, age 16

Appreciating
what's around you.
Hayley, age 14

Caring about others.
Ashley, age 16

My
friends!
Lilly – age 11

My best friend.
Chantel, age 14

Forgetting the bad stuff.
Josh, age 14

Making new
memories.
Chase, age 12

Making new friends.
Taisha, age 9

Happy Words:

Classic and Contemporary Quotes on Happiness

Mark Twain once said, "Whoever is happy
will make others happy, too." So in the interest
of sharing, here is a collection of thoughts on
happiness. From Balzac to Bill Cosby, see
what joyful wisdom others have gleaned...

To take heart in the simple pleasures
of each day...a patch of sunshine,
a baby's laugh, or the comfort of being
truly understood is to discover
the true happiness in life.

Linda Elrod

Every moment of life holds the potential for joy
that's just waiting to be released by a happy heart.

Lisa Riggin

We find a delight in the beauty and happiness of children that makes the heart too big for the body.

Ralph Waldo Emerson

Children laugh an average of 300 or more times a day.
Adults laugh an average of 17 times a day.
We have a lot of catching up to do.

Heather King

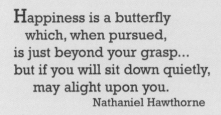

Happiness is a butterfly
which, when pursued,
is just beyond your grasp...
but if you will sit down quietly,
may alight upon you.
Nathaniel Hawthorne

Happiness is...
Keeping your spirit burning brightly,
Learning to take your troubles lightly,
Counting your blessings daily, nightly.
Linda Elrod

Life's truest happiness
is found in the friendships
we make along the way.
R. Bennett

Those who bring
happiness
to the lives of others
cannot keep it
from themselves.

Sir James Barrie

Live with your whole being...
all the days of your life!
Your reward will be true happiness!

Rebecca Thomas Shaw

Nothing I've ever done has
given me more joys and rewards
than being a father to my five.

Bill Cosby

Happiness is
when friends
remember your
birthday...
and forget
your age.

C. Myers

Happiness is a cat.
The way to pursue it is by acting like
you don't care if it comes to you or not.
And before you know it,
it's right there in your lap.
Myra Zirkle

You don't have to know everything to be happy — in fact, it helps.
Russ Ediger

Happiness is getting a brown gravy stain on a brown dress.
Totie Fields

The only way to live happily ever after
is to do it one day at a time.

Dean Walley

My father died at 102. Whenever
I would ask what kept him going,
he'd answer, "I never worry."
Jerry Stiller

The father who laughs
with his kids more than
he lectures them
is way ahead of the game.
Harry Stein

No day is so bad
that it can't be fixed with a nap.
Carrie Snow

To love what
you do and
feel that it
matters—
how could
anything be
more fun?

Katharine Graham.

When faced with a decision, I always ask,
"What would be the most fun?"
Peggy Walker

When he saw his daughters happy,
he knew he had done well.
Honoré de Balzac

Happiness
is a light
that spreads from
heart to heart.
Keely Chace

Happiness
is only a
hug
away!

Ginnie Job

Happy people

don't reach for happiness.
It's just something
that comes to them
when they are working and
exploring and dreaming
and giving life all they've got.
Happiness is a gift bestowed
on those who live and learn
and love to the fullest
every day of their lives.

Dean Walley

Perhaps one has to be very old before one learns
how to be amused rather than shocked.
Pearl S. Buck

Happiness
consists of
golden moments,
small in size
but great in meaning.
Renee Duvall

Don't get your
knickers in a knot.
Nothing is solved, and it just
makes you walk funny.
Kathryn Carpenter

Happiness makes its home
in hearts filled with love.
Jim Langdon

You are happiest
when you make
your own music
in your own way.

Linda Barnes

Money can't buy happiness.
But it CAN buy a

candy
necklace
at Woolworth's,
and that's pretty close.

John Dill

**Happy the life that is always spent
offering others encouragement.**

Kay Andrew

Happiness doesn't always just happen—
it comes as I discover
what is truly important in life.

Linda Staten

To be able to find

joy

in another's joy,
that is the secret
of happiness.

George Bernanos

Places and circumstances
never guarantee happiness.
You must decide within yourself
whether you want to be happy.

Robert J. Hastings

Happiness depends not upon
things around me, but on my

attitude.

Everything in my life
will depend on my attitude.

Alfred A. Montapert

The happiness that comes from doing
good is a happiness that will never end.
Chinese Proverb

To be without some of the things you want
is an indispensable part of happiness.
Bertrand Russell

One joy scatters a hundred griefs.
Chinese proverb

Though we travel the world over
to find the **beautiful**,
we must carry it with us
or we find it not.
Ralph Waldo Emerson

Happiness

always looks small
while you hold it
in your hands,
but let it go,
and you learn at
once how big
and **precious** it is.

Maksim Gorky

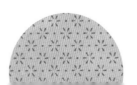

How happy are the pessimists!
What joy is theirs when they
have proved there is no joy."
Marie Ebner-Eschenbach

It's so important to know
that you can choose to
feel good.
Most people don't think
they have that choice.

Neil Simon

The grand essentials to happiness
in this life are
something to do,
someone to love,
and something to hope for.

Joseph Addison

Joy is never in our power and pleasure often is.
I doubt whether anyone who has tasted joy,
if both were in his power, would exchange it
for all the pleasure in the world.

C.S. Lewis

Having a child fall asleep
in your arms is one of the
most peaceful feelings in the world.
Andy Rooney

Happiness is where you find it.
Not finding it?
Perhaps you should look someplace else.
Bill Gray

If you want to be happy,
surround yourself with
happy people.
Cheryl Hawkinson

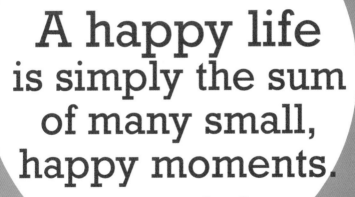

A happy life
is simply the sum
of many small,
happy moments.

Penny Krugman

Flowers know
that the key to
happiness
is to have a
little sunshine
on your face.

Jennifer Fujita

Happiness is an option,
not a given.
Exercise your options.
Kay Andrew

Happiness is a magical thing—
the more you share, the more
there is to go around.
Myra Zirkle

If you want the **rainbow**,
you gotta put up with the rain.
Dolly Parton

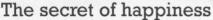

The secret of happiness

is not in doing what one likes to do,
but in liking what one has to do.

Sir James M. Barrie

Happiness seems

Success is getting what you want;
happiness is wanting what you get.

Charles F. Kettering

made to be shared.
Pierre Corneille

Where your pleasure is,
  there is your treasure.
Where your treasure is,
  there is your heart.
Where your heart is,
  there is your happiness.
St. Augustine

Happiness is not
a state to arrive at,
but a manner of traveling.
Margaret Lee Runbeck

The secret
of happiness is
freedom.
Thucydides

Unbroken happiness is a bore:
it should have ups and downs.
Molière

Happy is the day
when I can put a smile
on someone's face.
Scott Degelman

Happiness
is only
in loving.
Leo Tolstoy

If this book has made you—
or someone you care about—**happy**,
Hallmark would love to hear from you.
Please send your comments to:

Book Feedback

2501 McGee, Mail Drop 215

Kansas City, MO 64141-6580

Or email us at

booknotes@hallmark.com